WHERE DID THE WORLD COME FROM?

Genesis 1–3:15
for Children

Written and illustrated by
Karyn E. Lukasek

CONCORDIA PUBLISHING HOUSE · SAINT LOUIS

In the beginning, not much was around—
No people, no creatures, no trees, and no ground.
But God was there, and He had a great plan;
So work on the world in the darkness began . . .

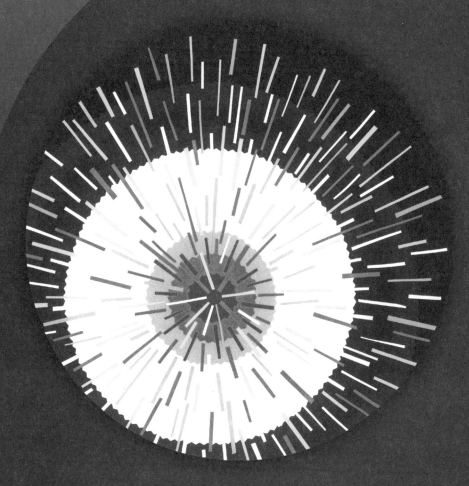

"Let there be light," our eternal God said;
So the darkness and light were separated.
The Father, the Son, and the Spirit agreed
That the light they created was good—good, indeed!

The darkness was *night*, and the light God called *day*,
To give us a time both to sleep and to play.
And there was evening and morning, the very first day.

Along with the darkness, the water was there.
Lots of it. Tons of it! Waves everywhere!
God's plan? He decided to split it in two;
Some water below, and some higher would do.

What went in the middle? God solved this one too!
The sky was created for me and for you.
And there was evening and morning, day number two.

Once the waters and sky had been properly placed,
Adding dry land was the next thing God faced.
His powerful Word made some dry ground appear,
And bodies of water, like seas, became clear.

The land produced veggies and fruits good for food,
Plus grasses and flowers and trees, for their wood;
These blessings God made on day three—
    they were good!

The plants God had put on the land needed light
To make their own seeds and to grow up all right.
So God made the sun to give light to the day,
While the moon and the stars shone
    at night far away.

The sky was content to be empty no more;
There'd be months now, and years,
    plus seasons galore!
God's power and goodness were clear on day four.

The sky was now ready for birds to fly in it;
Chirps, squawks, and coos filled the air in a minute!
There were black birds and brown birds
   and yellow and blue;
With long beaks and short beaks,
   and tails and wings too!

God's Word filled the waters with fish right away;
The seas were soon swimming with orange,
   blue, and gray.
Good were the creatures made on the fifth day.

The very next day, God filled up the land
With creatures that hop, climb, and dig in the sand;
Some furry, some fuzzy, some scaly, some sleek,
Some that howl or bark or bellow or squeak.

God saved His most special creation for last,
His love for all people especially vast.
He made Adam from dust, and from Adam made Eve.
He promised to bless them and never to leave.

From sin and from shame the first people were free—
They were made in God's wonderful image, you see;
These people and animals made day six busy!

Creation was finished, God's work was complete.

And He rested from working, His world now replete.

God blessed and sustained all the things He had made.

His laws were all good, and His people obeyed.

Of course, you might know that the story goes on:

Our first parents sinned, their holiness gone.

But God kept His promise to never leave them;

From their own sinful children the Savior would stem!

God had YOU in mind from creation, day one.

This world you live in took six days to be done,

And God has redeemed you through Jesus, His Son!

Dear Parent,

All children wonder about the natural world around them and about their place in it. The story of creation is the story of our heavenly Father's love for us, a love so vast that it is incomprehensible. Our eternal God *spoke* the world into existence out of nothing. For the child who persists in wondering how and why, this fact may be frustrating. When you read this book with your child, point out that while we can't understand how He did it, we can be sure of why: God created this marvelously beautiful world as a special place for us to live in. And He created each of us to have a special place in His world.

This book tells the biblical story of a six-day creation. We take the Genesis story literally because that's how God intends it. The Bible does not say that a *day* in Genesis is of indeterminate duration. And it does not say that when God made man, He did it by creating a single-celled organism that evolved over millions of years into a human being. Because He is who He is, God needed no longer than a blink of an eye to create the world and give it order—what we call *natural law*—and to put fully formed man in it as well.

The story of creation is also the story of our Lord's unbreakable covenant with us—that He would send a Savior from sin so we can be reconciled with Him and live with Him forever in paradise. From the beginning, it was God's intention to keep us close to Him. And through the death of His sinless Son, Jesus Christ, He does just that.

The Editor